MW01098794

Oats and Beans and Barley Grow

Retold by MEGAN BORGERT-SPANIOL

Illustrated by SHELAGH MCNICHOLAS with DAN CRISP

CANTATA
LEARNING
MANKATO, MINNESOTA

CANTATA LEARNING
MANKATO, MINNESOTA

Published by Cantata Learning
1710 Roe Crest Drive
North Mankato, MN 56003
www.cantatalearning.com

Library of Congress Control Number: 2014938333
ISBN: 978-1-63290-069-2

Oats and Beans and Barley Grow retold by Megan Borgert-Spaniol
Illustrated by Shelagh McNicholas with Dan Crisp

Book design by Tim Palin Creative
Music produced by Wes Schuck
Audio recorded, mixed, and mastered at Two Fish Studios, Mankato, MN

Printed in the United States of America.

VISIT
WWW.CANTATALEARNING.COM/ACCESS-OUR-MUSIC

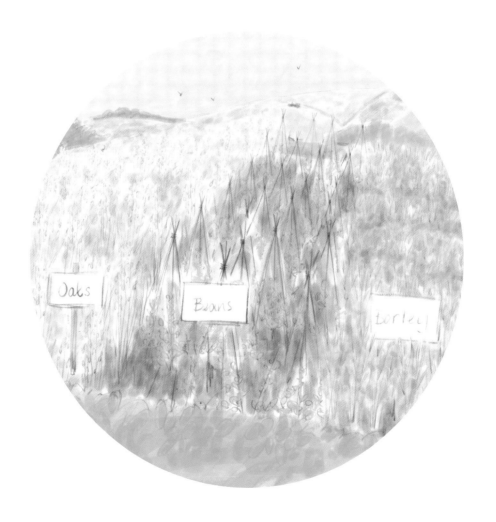

Farmers plant **crops** in their fields. The crops need water and sunlight to grow. Farmers use **hoes** to clear away **weeds**. Soon it is time to **harvest** the crops!

When you hear the sprinkler, turn the page.

Oats and beans and barley grow.

Oats and beans and barley grow.

Do you or I or anyone know
How oats and beans and barley grow?

First the farmer plants the seeds,
Stands up tall and takes his ease,
Stamps his foot and claps his hands,
And turns around to view his land.

Oats and beans and barley grow.

Oats and beans and barley grow.

Do you or I or anyone know
How oats and beans and barley grow?

Then the farmer waters the seeds,
Stands up tall and takes his ease,
Stamps his foot and claps his hands,
And turns around to view his land.

Oats and beans and barley grow.

Oats and beans and barley grow.

Do you or I or anyone know
How oats and beans and barley grow?

Next the farmer hoes the weeds,
Stands up tall and takes his ease,
Stamps his foot and claps his hands,
And turns around to view his land.

Oats and beans and barley grow.

Oats and beans and barley grow.

Do you or I or anyone know
How oats and beans and barley grow?

Oats

beans

barley

Last the farmer harvests the seeds,
Stands up tall and takes his ease,
Stamps his foot and claps his hands,
And turns around to view his land.

GLOSSARY

crops—plants that farmers grow

harvest—to pick or gather crops

hoes—tools that farmers use to clear weeds away from their crops

weeds—plants that get in the way and keep crops from growing

Oats and Beans and Barley Grow

Public Domain
Traditional

TO LEARN MORE

Bodach, Vijaya. *Seeds*. Mankato, MN: Capstone Press, 2007.

Dickmann, Nancy. *Plants on a Farm*. Chicago: Heinemann Library, 2011.

Goodman, Emily. *Plant Secrets*. Watertown, MA: Charlesbridge, 2009.

Nunn, Daniel. *Light*. Chicago: Heinemann Library, 2012.

Rattini, Kristin Baird. *National Geographic Readers: Seed to Plant*. Washington, DC: National Geographic Society, 2014.